7⁵⁰

To Anne and Patsy,
who love pigs!

Text copyright © 1986 Linda M. Jennings
Illustrations copyright © 1986 Krystyna Turska

First published 1986

First published by Hodder and Stoughton Children's Books,
a division of Hodder and Stoughton Ltd,
Mill Road, Dunton Green, Sevenoaks, Kent TN13 2YJ

Published in the United States in 1986 by
Silver Burdett Company
Morristown, New Jersey

Library of Congress Cataloging-in-Publication Data
Jennings, Linda M.
  Crispin and the dancing piglet.

  Summary: His father and older brothers laugh when,
out of all the animals on the farm, Crispin chooses
to take a tiny piglet with him when he goes out into
the world to seek his fortune.
  [1. Pigs—Fiction] I. Turska, Krystyna, 1933– ill.
II. Title.
PZ7.J42985Cr 1986 [E]   86–1968
ISBN 0-382-09242-2

Printed in Belgium

Crispin and The Dancing Piglet

written by Linda M. Jennings

illustrated by Krystyna Turska

SILVER BURDETT
MORRISTOWN, NEW JERSEY

Once there was a wealthy farmer who had three sons. Fine, strong lads they were, and every year, from seedtime till harvest, they helped their father on the farm, until the day came when the farmer decided to send them all out into the world to seek their fortunes.

To help them on their way he promised each a golden sovereign and the choice of any animal on the farm.

"Well, I will choose your magnificent black stallion,"
said Thomas, the eldest, "for from him I can breed horses
fit for the King himself."

Now Michael, the second son, had decided to become a merchant.
"And so I shall need a faithful but fierce hound to guard my fortunes,"
he said.

But Crispin, the youngest son, chose a tiny, tiny piglet,
the runt of the litter.

His brothers laughed until they cried.

"All *he's* good for is bacon," they jeered,
"and a mighty small meal he'd make, too!"

Crispin took no notice of his brothers' taunts. The very next day he watched his two brothers leave the farm, one prancing off on the proud black stallion, the other followed by a huge hound, snarling protectively behind him. Then Crispin took his little piglet and scrubbed him till he glowed pink as the sunset and polished his hooves till they shone like black diamonds.

"I shall call you Marmaduke," he said.

Tucking the piglet under his arm Crispin set off along the highway.

At midday he stopped at a wayside inn and, breaking into his sovereign, he ordered himself some bread and cheese and a pint of ale, and for Marmaduke a big bowl of buttered potatoes.

The landlord was horrified. "Why, I have plenty of swill in the yard – I can let you have it free," he said.

"Only the best for my pig," said Crispin. "For treat him like a pig and he'll behave like a pig."

It was a fine spring afternoon with the hint of a breeze. Presently Crispin began to skip a little, for he was very happy, traveling on under the blue sky, free as air.

To his surprise Marmaduke, who had been trotting at his heels, did the same.
Next Crispin danced a jig in the middle of the road.
Marmaduke did the same.
"Bless me," cried Crispin in delight. "I have a dancing piglet!"

Towards nightfall the two of them reached the Town that Lay Under the Mountains.

After all their dancing Crispin and his piglet were very tired indeed but alas, the town was completely full because the next day there was to be the Annual Fair. From door to door they went, seeking a room.

At last they reached a snug-looking cottage on the edge of the town.
The door was opened by a fierce-looking woman with a rolling pin.

"No pigs in this house," she cried, when Crispin wearily repeated
his request for a room. "The very idea – be off with you!"

At this Marmaduke stood up on his little back hooves,
bowed, and danced a minuet in the yard.

The woman stared and stared.

"He can dance for his supper – and his bed," said Crispin.

"Well, there's a sight," said the woman, and
opened the door to both of them.

The next day all the town was busy preparing for the Fair. Crispin, too, was up early, staring at all the sights, and planning what to do with his remarkable pig.

Presently, he bought a little reed pipe and, with Marmaduke at his heels, walked to the nearby river bank. Here he sat all day practicing his tunes, while Marmaduke danced and waltzed and jigged to the music.

As evening drew near,
the people came from
all around the town and nearby villages to
enjoy the Fair. Such a festive crowd it was
that listened to the music
and stared at all the decorated stalls –
and at the sight of a young country lad
who played his reed pipe so jauntily
that his little pig waltzed
and jumped and even did the polka,
for the sheer joy of it.

"What a beautiful little pig!"

"He's so *dainty!*"

"What I would do to own a little
pig like that."

Very soon money began to pour into
the open bag that lay at Crispin's feet,
and when at last the streets emptied
and the stalls closed the boy found
he had made a small fortune.

Crispin and Marmaduke traveled on and on from fair to fair, from town to town,
and in each place their performance was greeted with cries of delight and showers of money.
Another remarkable thing about Marmaduke was that he never grew any bigger than he was
on the day Crispin took him from the sty. Many wanted to buy the little pig, but
Crispin was not tempted by the offers of bags of gold, fine houses,
or trips to far-off countries beyond the sea.

One day they happened to visit the capital
on the very occasion of the Princess's birthday.
Now this Princess was very spoiled, and
though she had received many beautiful presents
none really pleased her.

The King, however, had heard of Crispin
and his dancing piglet, and ordered them
to appear at the Palace in the hope that
their performance might entertain his daughter.

Indeed it did. The Princess was enchanted,
and, clapping her hands, she cried:

"Oh, what a *darling* little pig.
I must have him for my very own."

But Crispin refused to part
with his pig, as he had many
times before.

The Princess was so furious at his refusal that she began to pout and cry and demand the little pig.

The King shook his head sadly. "Alas, young man, I must order you to part with your pig, much as you love him. For if my daughter doesn't get her way she will stamp and scream around the Palace for days."

What could poor Crispin do?

"Take care of him, won't you," he said to the Princess, with tears in his eyes.

"*Of course,*" said the Princess. "Why, he'll sleep in my bedroom on a silken cushion, and eat marshmallows, and dance on my marble mantelpiece."

But it immediately became apparent that Marmaduke would do none of these things the Princess had planned for him. From the moment that the Princess took the piglet from Crispin he began to grow…

AND GROW...

AND GROW...

AND GROW... AND GROW...

until the Princess sat down hard on her bottom under the weight of him.
She burst into tears. "I don't want a huge beast like that," she cried.
"Take him away at once!"

As soon as Crispin led Marmaduke from the Palace
the pig shrank to his usual dainty size.
After that time, if anyone tried to steal
or trick Marmaduke away from his master
(and several did) – well, you know what happened!

What of Crispin's two brothers? Well, Thomas did indeed breed horses for the King –
and he married the King's daughter, too. But we have met her already,
so you can imagine how happy *he* was!

Michael became the richest man in the whole country. He was also the loneliest,
for the hound was so fierce that none dared approach him,
not even the gentlest and fairest women in the land.

As for Crispin – why, he married a fresh-faced country girl,
who looked after Marmaduke with as much loving care
as she did her husband,
and fed him with a huge bowl of
buttered potatoes every day.